little Miss Late

by Roger Hargreaves

Late for this.

Late for that.

Little Miss Late was late for everything!

For instance.

Do you know where she spent last Christmas?

At home.

Earlybird Cottage!

But, do you know when she spent Christmas?

January 25th!

One month late!

For example.

Do you know when she did her spring cleaning at Earlybird Cottage?

In the summer!

Three months late!

For instance.

Do you know when she went on her summer holiday last year?

In December!

Six months late!

Earlybird Cottage was just along the road from where a friend of hers lived.

Little Miss Neat.

Little Miss Neat was out for an evening stroll last October when she looked over the hedge of Earlybird Cottage.

Miss Late was in the garden.

"Hello," called out Little Miss Neat. "What are you doing?"

"I thought I'd cut the grass!" replied Miss Late.

"I think," remarked Little Miss Neat, looking at the grass, "that you should have thought about that last April!"

"Tell you what," suggested Miss Neat. "Let's go shopping together tomorrow!"

"Good idea," agreed Miss Late.

"I'll meet you in town on the corner of Main Street tomorrow afternoon," said Miss Neat.

"Two o'clock!"

"I'll be there," replied Miss Late.

The following afternoon Little Miss Neat stood on the corner of Main Street at two o'clock.

Waiting for Miss Late.

She waited.

And waited.

And waited some more.

Miss Late arrived.

"Sorry I'm a bit late," she apologised.

"Sorry?" cried Miss Neat. "A bit late? It's five o'clock and all the shops are shut!!"

"Sorry," said Miss Late.

And that's what happened, all the time!

It happened when Miss Late decided to take a job.

Her first job was in a bank.

But the trouble was, by the time she arrived for work, the bank had closed for the day.

Every day!

"Sorry," she said.

They asked her to leave.

It happened in her second job, as a waitress in a restaurant.

Mr Greedy came in for lunch.

He glanced at the menu.

"I'll have everything," he grinned.

"Twice!"

He was still waiting to be served at seven o'clock.

So he went home.

"Sorry," said Little Miss Late.

They asked her to leave.

It happened in her third job, working as a secretary for Mr Uppity.

"I'd like these letters typed before I go home," Mr Uppity said to her.
He went home at four o'clock.

In the morning!

"Sorry," said Little Miss Late.

He asked her to leave.

However, as it happened, which is often the way of things, Little Miss Late managed to find herself the perfect job.

She now works for Mr Lazy!

She cooks and cleans for him.

Cleaning his house every morning.

Cooking his lunch every lunchtime.

Now.

Mr Lazy, being Mr Lazy, doesn't get up in the morning like you and I do.

He gets up in the afternoon!

And Little Miss Late, being Little Miss Late, is always late for work.

So she doesn't arrive for work in the morning.

She arrives in the afternoon!

And.

Mr Lazy, being Mr Lazy, doesn't have lunch at lunchtime like you and I do.

He has lunch at suppertime!

And so you see it all works very well.

Very well indeed!

Last Friday evening the telephone rang in Earlybird Cottage.

Little Miss Late had just arrived home from work.

It was Mr Silly on the telephone.

"I've been given some tickets for a dance tomorrow night," he said.

"Would you like to come?"

"Oo, yes please," said Miss Late eagerly.

"Right," replied Mr Silly.

"I'll pick you up at seven o'clock!"

Last Saturday Mr Silly walked up the path to the front door of Earlybird Cottage.

He knocked.

"Come in," called a voice from upstairs.

Mr Silly went in.

"Make yourself at home," called Little Miss Late from upstairs.

"I'll be down in a minute!"

Fantastic offers for Little Miss fans!

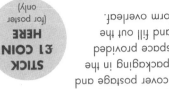

Collect all your Mr. Men or Little Miss books in these superb durable collectors' cases!

Only £5.99 inc. postage and packing, these wipe-clean, hard-wearing cases will give all your Mr. Men or Little Miss books a beautiful new home!

Keep track of your collection with this giant-sized double-sided Mr. Men and Little Miss Collectors' poster.

Collect 6 tokens and we will send you a brilliant giant-sized double-sided collectors' poster! Simply tape a £1 coin to cover postage and packaging in the space provided and fill out the form overleaf.

STICK £1 COIN HERE (for poster only)

1 TOKEN · LITTLE MISS · 1 TOKEN

Only need a few Little Miss or Mr. Men to complete your set? You can order any of the titles on the back of the books from our Mr. Men order line on 0870 787 1724. Orders should be delivered between 5 and 7 working days.

— TO BE COMPLETED BY AN ADULT —

To apply for any of these great offers, ask an adult to complete the details below and send this whole page with the appropriate payment and tokens, to: MR. MEN CLASSIC OFFER, PO BOX 715, HORSHAM RH12 5WG

☐ Please send me a giant-sized double-sided collectors' poster.

AND ☐ I enclose 6 tokens and have taped a £1 coin to the other side of this page.

☐ Please send me ☐ Mr. Men library case(s) and/or ☐ Little Miss library case(s) at £5.99 each inc P&P

☐ I enclose a cheque/postal order payable to Egmont UK Limited for £

OR ☐ Please debit my MasterCard / Visa / Maestro / Delta account (delete as appropriate) for £

Card no. ☐☐☐☐☐☐☐☐☐☐☐☐☐☐☐☐   Security code ☐☐☐

Issue no. (if available) ☐☐   Start Date ☐☐/☐☐   Expiry Date ☐☐/☐☐

Fan's name: ....   Date of birth: ....

Address: ....

....

Postcode: ....

Name of parent / guardian: ....

Email for parent / guardian: ....

Signature of parent / guardian: ....

Please allow 28 days for delivery. Offer is only available while stocks last. We reserve the right to change the terms of this offer at any time and we offer a 14 day money back guarantee. This does not affect your statutory rights. Offers apply to UK only.

☐ We may occasionally wish to send you information about other Egmont children's books.
☐ If you would rather we didn't, please tick this box.

Ref: LIM 001

cut along the dotted line and return this whole page